MY YOM TOV ALBUM

MY YOM TOV ALBUM

ALBUM

MY YOM TOV ALBUM

MY YOM TOV ALBUM

MY YOM TOV ALBUM

MY YOM TOV ALBUM

MY YOM TOV ALBUM

MY YOM TOV ALBUM

MY YOM TOV ALBUM

MY YOM TOV ALBUM

MY YOM TOV ALBUM

MY YOM TOV ALBUM

MY YOM TOV ALBUM

MY YOM TOV ALBUM

MY YOM TOV ALBUM

MY YOM TOV ALBUM

My YOM TOV Album

Z. Pfeffer

Enjoyable and enriching reading

Translated into English by
Ruth Steinberg

My YOM TOV Album

Written, Designed, and Illustrated by *Z. Pfeffer*

ISBN 1-931681-58-9

Distributed by:
Israel Book Shop
501 Prospect Street, Lakewood, NJ 08701

Tel: (732) 901-3009 Fax: (732) 901-4012
Email: isrbkshp@aol.com

Printed in Israel 5764 / 2004

בס"ד

My Yom Tov Album

My Yom Tov Album, originally published in Hebrew, is now available to English-speaking Jewish children.

The book portrays the yearly cycle of Jewish holidays in the form of brief, beautifully illustrated, descriptions in verse. These portrayals convey a variety of educational values, and the highlights of the various laws and customs are ideal for young readers.

Accompanying each illustrated story are familiar prayers and blessings, along with their sources and a brief explanation. This material can be easily expanded upon by both parents and teachers and serves as an enjoyable introduction to and /or review of a vital topic that is an integral part of our children's lives.

בס"ד עש"ק לסדר **ויצא פרח ויצץ ציץ** התשנ'ו לב"ע

Erev Shabbos kodesh parashas Korach, 5756

Life, peace and all the best always to my dear and very esteemed friend, crowned with courtesy, a delicate soul of refined character, kind and benevolent--Rabbi Zishe Pfeffer, may he and his entire family enjoy a good and pleasant life.

Greetings of affection and friendship. I was happy to see the book *Chagei Yisrael*, which you are about to reprint and disseminate among Jewish children. It is certainly of great importance to instill knowledge of the delight and sanctity of the holidays from an early age.

Our holy Torah was given with the word "*Anochi*" (I [am Hashem, your God...]). Our Sages explain [the letters of "*Anochi*" as an acrostic] in Gemara *Shabbos* (105a): " 'I Myself have given this writing.' The Rabbis say, 'Pleasant words given in writing.' Others reverse the letters: 'Rendered faithfully into writing.' "

The giving of our holy Torah began with "*Anochi*" to allude to the aforementioned [idea]. Certainly, then, the concepts of the sacred holidays throughout the year should be presented to children pleasantly and faithfully, in sanctity and in an attractive manner, [so these ideas] will be preserved. This is especially true of material learned in childhood. Rashi explains: "[It] is retained more than [what is learned] when old (see *Shabbos* 21b)." And [these concepts] demand great exactitude, so they will be preserved correctly and properly.

It is obvious how much work and effort went into this book, for it's well-done and succinct, and one should always teach students succinctly, especially children. *Baruch Hashem*, you have produced a fine, high-quality volume that will greatly benefit all the children who study it.

We find that the mitzvah of *Hakhel* on Sukkos (*Vayeilech* 31:12) was to assemble the nation: "men, women, and children... so they will hear and learn." The holidays have a particular educational power and should be utilized for that purpose.

The Gemara *Chagigah* (3a) asks: Why did the children come? The Gemara answers: To give reward to those who brought them. This book will surely be of great benefit to children, so they will hear and learn.

And you, who "bring them," certainly deserve great reward in this world, with the principal preserved for the World to Come. May you merit "the reward of one mitzvah is another," and further endeavors for "Torah and testimony," in keeping with your wishes and those of one who seeks your benefit and well-being from the depths of his heart.

Written and signed with sincere and loyal feelings of blessings and friendship.

Rabbi B.Z. Rabinowitz

Rabbi B.Z. Rabinowitz
OF BIALA
Sorotzkin 47 Str.
JERUSALEM

בן ציון רבינוביץ
בלאאמו"ר זצוקללה"ה
מביאלא
רח' סורוצקין 47 ירושלים

בס"ד [illegible] התשנ"ו, לב"ע

[illegible]

בן ציון רבינוביץ בלאאמו"ר זצוקללה"ה מביאלא.

בש"ס בן ציון רבינוביץ
בלאאמו"ר
מביאלא
זצוקלל"ה
אב"ד דק"ק לוגאנא

ROSH HASHANAH

ROSH HASHANAH

ROSH HASHANAH

Rosh Hashanah is on the 1st and 2nd of Tishrei

Rising Early for *Selichos*

The world is asleep; it is not yet day,
But the Jewish people are going to pray.
On these special days when Hashem is so near,
We ask for forgiveness and know He will hear.
Selichos is the time to repent – start again;
For all – young and old, women and men.
All are determined to make a new start,
To return to Hashem with a *Teshuvah* - filled heart.
Even small children want to be good,
They try to act, as they know they should.
The sky is still dark and the air is cool,
As we go together to daven in shul.
There the *Chazan* prays aloud and all join as one,
Begging Hashem to forgive what we've done.

סְלַח לָנוּ אָבִינוּ כִּי חָטָאנוּ, מְחַל לָנוּ מַלְכֵּנוּ כִּי פָשָׁעְנוּ, כִּי אַתָּה ה'
טוֹב וְסַלָּח וְרַב – חֶסֶד לְכָל קֹרְאֶךָ.

Forgive us, our Father, for *aveiros* we have done by
mistake; pardon us, our King, for we have sinned on
purpose; for You, Hashem, are good and forgiving and
very kind to all who call upon You.

The main part of *Selichos* is the Thirteen Attributes of Hashem's Mercy, followed by
our prayer: "Forgive us, our Father... pardon us, our King..."

2
ROSH HASHANAH

Rosh Hashanah is on the 1st and 2nd of Tishrei

New Year Greetings

Our little sister is still very small,
But she wants to be ahead of us all.
"It's my turn now," her smile seems to say,
As she stretches her arm our father's way.
But then she looks down and starts to cry –
Big Brother's first, and she doesn't know why.
Our father blesses us each, as the new year starts,
With a few special words, which touch our hearts.
Our mother quietly wipes away a tear,
As she wishes us all a good new year!
They *bentch* each member of the *mishpachah*,
With these special words - a heartfelt *brachah*:

*For men and boys:

לְשָׁנָה טוֹבָה תִּכָּתֵב וְתֵחָתֵם לְאַלְתַּר לְחַיִּים טוֹבִים וּלְשָׁלוֹם.

*For women and girls:

לְשָׁנָה טוֹבָה תִּכָּתֵבִי וְתֵחָתֵמִי לְאַלְתַּר לְחַיִּים טוֹבִים וּלְשָׁלוֹם.

May you be inscribed and sealed immediately for a good
life and for peace.

When writing a letter in Elul, we add the words "*Ani Ledodi Vedodi Li*," which begin
with the initials of אלול and mean: We are close to Hashem, and Hashem is close to us.

3
ROSH HASHANAH

Rosh Hashanah is on the 1st and 2nd of Tishrei

The Simanim (Symbolic Foods)

For Rosh Hashanah we cook and bake
Special food and delicious cake.
The table is set with extra care
And the finest Mommy can prepare.
There are apples and honey, dates and fish,
With a hint in the name of each special dish.
We say *Yehi Ratzon* before each food we eat,
Asking Hashem for a year that is sweet.
These prayers are said only once a year,
We repeat after our father, loud and clear:

May it be Your will, Hashem, our G-d and the G-d of our forefathers,

יְהִי רָצוֹן מִלְפָנֶיךָ ה' אֱ–לֹקֵינוּ וֵא–לֹקֵי אֲבוֹתֵינוּ:

*

Dates (*Tamar*):

that our enemies meet their end.

שֶׁיִּתַּמּוּ שׂוֹנְאֵינוּ וְאוֹיְבֵינוּ.

*

Pomegranate (*Rimon*):

that our merits increase like (the seeds of) a pomegranate.

שֶׁנַּרְבֶּה זְכֻיּוֹת כְּרִמּוֹן.

*

Apple dipped in honey:

that You renew for us a good, sweet year.

שֶׁתְּחַדֵּשׁ עָלֵינוּ שָׁנָה טוֹבָה וּמְתוּקָה.

*

Gourd (*Kara*):

that our evil decree be canceled; and may our merits be proclaimed before You.

שֶׁתִּקְרַע רֹעַ גְּזַר דִּינֵנוּ, וְיִקָּרְאוּ לְפָנֶיךָ זְכֻיּוֹתֵינוּ.

*

Black-eyed peas (*Rubia*):

that our merits increase.

שֶׁיִּרְבּוּ זְכֻיּוֹתֵינוּ.

*

Leek or cabbage (*Karti*):

that our enemies be wiped out.

שֶׁיִּכָּרְתוּ שׂוֹנְאֵינוּ.

*

Beets (*Silka*):

that our foes be removed.

שֶׁיִּסְתַּלְקוּ שׂוֹנְאֵינוּ.

*

Head of fish (or sheep):

that we be like the head and not like the tail.

שֶׁנִּהְיֶה לְרֹאשׁ וְלֹא לְזָנָב.

Our Sages said, "Symbols have meaning," and they can influence us, so on the night of Rosh Hashanah, we eat special foods whose names hint at good.

4
ROSH HASHANAH

Rosh Hashanah is on the 1st and 2nd of Tishrei

Blowing the Shofar

"Hashem is King," everyone proclaims,
"Of the entire world and all it contains.
But above all," continues our declaration,
"Hashem is King of the Jewish nation."
The shofar is covered, not a word is spoken,
Then the blessings are said and the silence is broken.
The Satan is confused when the shofar is blown,
And we pray before the Heavenly Throne.
Our hearts are filled with awe and fear,
As Hashem judges us for the coming year.
Hashem's mercy is stirred by the shofar's blast,
And He forgives us for the sins of the past.

Before blowing, the *ba'al toke'a* says "*Alah Elokim Biteruah...*," and makes these blessings:

בָּרוּךְ אַתָּה ה', אֱ–לֹקֵינוּ מֶלֶךְ הָעוֹלָם, אֲשֶׁר קִדְּשָׁנוּ בְּמִצְוֹתָיו,
וְצִוָּנוּ לִשְׁמֹעַ קוֹל שׁוֹפָר.

Blessed are You, Hashem, our G-d, King of the universe, Who has sanctified us with His commandments and commanded us to hear the sound of the shofar.

בָּרוּךְ אַתָּה ה', אֱ–לֹקֵינוּ מֶלֶךְ הָעוֹלָם, שֶׁהֶחֱיָנוּ וְקִיְּמָנוּ וְהִגִּיעָנוּ
לַזְּמַן הַזֶּה.

Blessed are You, Hashem, our G-d, King of the universe, Who has kept us alive, sustained us, and brought us to this season.

Blowing a ram's horn reminds us of *Akeidas Yitzchak,* which took place on Rosh Hashanah. Yitzchak agreed to be sacrificed, but a ram was slaughtered in his place.

Rosh Hashanah is on the 1st and 2nd of Tishrei

Tashlich

On Rosh Hashanah, late in the day,
There's a very special *Tefilah* that we say.
We go to a river, a pond, or a lake,
Where fish swim about; our *machzorim* we take.
But if there's no river or lake nearby,
There's somewhere else that we can try.
At a well filled with water, we can also pray
That Hashem cast our *aveiros* away.
We ask that He help us learn Torah day and night,
And that we should be able to do only what is right.
Then we shake out the corners of our clothes
Into the water which peacefully flows.

We say this prayer on the first day of Rosh Hashanah.
(If it is Shabbos, we say it on the second day.)

מִי־אֵ־ל כָּמוֹךָ, נֹשֵׂא עָוֹן וְעֹבֵר עַל־פֶּשַׁע לִשְׁאֵרִית נַחֲלָתוֹ, לֹא־
הֶחֱזִיק לָעַד אַפּוֹ, כִּי־חָפֵץ חֶסֶד הוּא. יָשׁוּב יְרַחֲמֵנוּ, יִכְבֹּשׁ עֲוֹנֹתֵינוּ,
וְתַשְׁלִיךְ בִּמְצֻלוֹת יָם כָּל־חַטֹּאתָם.

Who, Hashem, is like You, pardoning the sins and wrongdoing of the remnant of His people? He does not remain angry forever, because He wants to deal kindly with us. He will again be merciful to us; He will hold back our wrongdoing and cast all our sins into the depths of the sea.

When Avraham went to sacrifice Yitzchak, the Satan appeared to them in the form of a river, to stop them. We say *Tashlich* near water as a reminder of Avraham's willingness to sacrifice his son.

YOM KIPPUR

YOM KIPPUR

YOM KIPPUR

Yom Kippur is on the 10th of Tishrei

Kapparos

MY YOM TOV ALBUM

Our mother brought home a surprise last night;
Two live chickens, both creamy white.
"The rooster," she said, "is for the men,
But the girls and I will use the hen.
Some use fish for *Kapparos,* some use money –
We follow the *minhag* of our family."
This morning, one chicken became untied;
The baby was frightened and wanted to hide.
Mommy gently calmed him and brought him back in,
Then she picked up a chicken; it was time to begin!
Over our heads, the chickens we whirl,
With a special *Tefilah* for each boy and girl.

The rooster or hen is swung over the head, and the following is said three times:

*For men and boys:

זֶה חֲלִיפָתִי, זֶה תְּמוּרָתִי, זֶה כַּפָּרָתִי, זֶה הַתַּרְנְגוֹל יֵלֵךְ לְמִיתָה, וַאֲנִי אֶכָּנֵס וְאֵלֵךְ לְחַיִּים טוֹבִים אֲרוּכִים וּלְשָׁלוֹם.

This is my exchange, this is my substitute, this is my atonement. This rooster will go to its death, while I will enter and go to a good, long life, and to peace.

*For women and girls:

זֹאת חֲלִיפָתִי, זֹאת תְּמוּרָתִי, זֹאת כַּפָּרָתִי, זֹאת הַתַּרְנְגֹלֶת תֵּלֵךְ לְמִיתָה, וַאֲנִי אֶכָּנֵס וְאֵלֵךְ לְחַיִּים טוֹבִים אֲרוּכִים וּלְשָׁלוֹם.

This is my exchange, this is my substitute, this is my atonement. This hen will go to its death, while I will enter and go to a good, long life, and to peace.

Before Yom Kippur, the *Kapparos* (chicken, fish, or money) are given to charity, because *Teshuvah*, *Tefilah*, and *Tzedakah* cancel harsh *gezeiros*.

Yom Kippur is on the 10th of Tishrei

The *Seudah Hamafsekes*

Mommy is busy cooking a meal today,
But the food is not for Yom Kippur – no way!
On Erev Yom Kippur, it's a mitzvah to eat,
We have a *seudah* with chicken or meat.
The *Seudah Hamafsekes* must end right on time,
We all drink enough, so we should feel fine.
We fast on Yom Kippur; there's no eating then,
From age twelve for women, from thirteen for men.
Youngsters break their fast in the middle;
They get used to fasting little by little –
A bit more each year, as they grow strong,
Until they can fast all Yom Kippur long.

"וְעִנִּיתֶם אֶת־נַפְשֹׁתֵיכֶם בְּתִשְׁעָה"

"And you will afflict yourselves on the ninth (of Tishrei)."

Do we fast on the ninth? We fast on the tenth! We learn from this that whoever eats and drinks on the ninth and fasts on the tenth is considered by the Torah as if he fasted on *both* the ninth and tenth.

Eating, drinking, bathing, using oils or lotions, and wearing leather shoes are all forbidden on Yom Kippur. We wash our hands only until the knuckles.

3 YOM KIPPUR

Yom Kippur is on the 10th of Tishrei

Blessing the Children

The house is filled with awe and fear;
It's Erev Yom Kippur, and sunset draws near.
Everyone is ready – the work is all done.
Our father will *bentch* each daughter and son.
Oldest to youngest, we stand in line,
As our father *bentches* us, one at a time.
Tears fill our baby brother's eyes–
He's last in line, and so, he cries.
He buries his face in his chubby hands,
"Please *bentch* me first!" is what he demands.
Our mother, too, sheds silent tears,
As we are all blessed for a sweet new year.

*For boys:

יְשִׂמְךָ אֱ–לֹקִים כְּאֶפְרַיִם וְכִמְנַשֶּׁה;

יְבָרֶכְךָ ה' וְיִשְׁמְרֶךָ, יָאֵר ה' פָּנָיו אֵלֶיךָ וִיחֻנֶּךָּ, יִשָּׂא ה' פָּנָיו
אֵלֶיךָ וְיָשֵׂם לְךָ שָׁלוֹם...

May G-d make you like Efraim and Menasheh. May Hashem bless you and protect you. May Hashem shine His face toward you and be gracious to you. May Hashem turn His face to you and grant you peace.

*For girls:

יְשִׂמֵךְ אֱ–לֹקִים כְּשָׂרָה, כְּרִבְקָה, כְּרָחֵל וּכְלֵאָה.

May G-d make you like Sarah, Rivkah, Rachel, and Leah.

Before Yom Kippur, when our judgment will be sealed, parents tearfully bless their children.

Yom Kippur is on the 10th of Tishrei

Kol Nidrei

A special *Kedushah* fills the air,
Soon all the shuls are ready for prayer.
Serious and still, we all search our hearts,
As we patiently wait for *Kol Nidrei* to start.
Before the sun sets, we annul every vow,
That was made throughout the year, until now.
And if we mistakenly make vows in the year ahead,
They are canceled already by this *Tefilah* we've said.
The *chazan* and two men, all dressed in white,
Hold *sifrei Torah* and hug them tight.
The *chazan* begins, his voice deep and strong;
We all join in and daven along:

כָּל נִדְרֵי וֶאֱסָרֵי וּשְׁבוּעֵי וַחֲרָמֵי... בְּטֵלִין וּמְבֻטָּלִין, לָא שְׁרִירִין וְלָא
קַיָּמִין. נִדְרָנָא לָא נִדְרֵי וֶאֱסָרָנָא לָא אֱסָרֵי וּשְׁבוּעָתָנָא לָא שְׁבוּעוֹת.

All vows and oaths... are completely canceled, not in effect, and nonexistent. The vows are not vows, and the oaths are not oaths.

Vows are not canceled on Shabbos or holidays (unless necessary for the same day).
This is why *Kol Nidrei* is said on *erev Yom Kippur* before sunset.

YOM KIPPUR

Yom Kippur is on the 10th of Tishrei

Viduy (Confession)

Regret is the way *Teshuvah* begins,
Then we have to admit to all of our sins.
But before we say *viduy*, sentence by sentence,
Let's thank Hashem for the gift of repentance.
Every person can truly change his ways,
And resolve to do good for the rest of his days!
"We've done wrong," we say, as we pound our hearts,
This is the way that our *viduy* starts.
We list our *aveiros*, forgetting none,
We admit to them all, one by one.
With broken hearts, we hope and pray,
That Hashem will accept our *Tefilos* today.

עַל חֵטְא שֶׁחָטָאנוּ לְפָנֶיךָ בְּזִלְזוּל הוֹרִים וּמוֹרִים;

For the *aveirah* we have done before You by showing disrespect for parents and teachers.

עַל חֵטְא שֶׁחָטָאנוּ לְפָנֶיךָ בְּלָשׁוֹן הָרָע;

For the *aveirah* we have done before You through *lashon hara* (evil talk).

וְעַל חֵטְא שֶׁחָטָאנוּ לְפָנֶיךָ בְּשִׂנְאַת חִנָם.

For the *aveirah* we have done before You with *sinas chinam* (baseless hatred).

וְעַל כֻּלָּם, אֱ–לוֹק סְלִיחוֹת, סְלַח לָנוּ, מְחַל לָנוּ, כַּפֶּר לָנוּ.

For them all, G-d of forgiveness, forgive us, pardon us, atone for us!

All Jews are responsible for one another. That's why the *viduy* (confession) is written in the plural: "*We* have become guilty, *we* have betrayed..."

SUKKOS

SUKKOS

Sukkos begins on the 15th of Tishrei

The Mitzvah of Sukkah

We're building a sukkah with hammers and saws;
But we must make sure that we know all the laws.
So first we will learn and study hard,
Before we start working in our backyard.
Although the sukkah's not a home for all year long,
Through wind and rain, our sukkah must stand strong!
Its roof is of branches detached from a tree,
This roof of *s'chach* must be made carefully.
It must be shady inside when the sun shines bright,
And we should see the stars through the *s'chach* at night.
When we enter the sukkah, there's a *Tefilah* to say,
And a *Yehi Ratzon* when we leave it on the last day.

*When entering the sukkah on the first night of Sukkos, we say:

הֲרֵינִי מוּכָן וּמְזֻמָּן לְקַיֵּם מִצְוַת סֻכָּה, כַּאֲשֶׁר צִוַּנִי הַבּוֹרֵא
יִתְבָּרַךְ שְׁמוֹ, "בַּסֻּכֹּת תֵּשְׁבוּ שִׁבְעַת יָמִים..."

Behold, I am prepared and ready to perform the commandment of the sukkah as the Creator, blessed is His Name, has commanded me: "You shall dwell in sukkos for seven days..."

*When leaving the sukkah on the last day of Sukkos, we say:

יְהִי רָצוֹן מִלְּפָנֶיךָ ה' אֱ–לֹקַי וֵא–לֹקֵי אֲבוֹתַי, כְּשֵׁם שֶׁקִּיַּמְתִּי וְיָשַׁבְתִּי
בְּסֻכָּה זוֹ, כֵּן אֶזְכֶּה לַשָּׁנָה הַבָּאָה לֵישֵׁב בְּסֻכַּת עוֹרוֹ שֶׁל לִוְיָתָן.

May it be Your will, Hashem, our G-d and the G-d of our forefathers, that just as I have fulfilled the mitzvah and sat in this sukkah, may I be worthy in the coming year to sit in the sukkah of the skin of *Livyasan* (Leviathan).

The sukkah reminds us of the Clouds of Glory, which protected the Jews in the desert: "Because I settled the Jewish People in sukkos when I took them out of Egypt."

Sukkos begins on the 15th of Tishrei

Decorating the Sukkah

Mommy is working hard to make
Delicious meals and special cakes.
She's preparing for Sukkos in many ways,
Our father is also quite busy these days.
We know it's a pleasure and a duty
To make the sukkah a place of beauty.
So we take charge of decorating,
The sukkah that we finished making.
Our mother and father are both surprised
At the lovely sight that greets their eyes.
"It's beautiful!" they proudly say.
"It's our new home for seven days."
All meals will be eaten in our sukkah,
And each time, we will say this *brachah*:

בָּרוּךְ אַתָּה ה', אֱ–לֹקֵינוּ מֶלֶךְ הָעוֹלָם, אֲשֶׁר קִדְּשָׁנוּ בְּמִצְוֹתָיו,
וְצִוָּנוּ לֵישֵׁב בַּסֻּכָּה.

Blessed are You, Hashem, our G-d, King of the universe,
Who has sanctified us with His commandments and
commanded us to dwell in the sukkah.

*On the first night, we add this blessing:

בָּרוּךְ אַתָּה ה', אֱ–לֹקֵינוּ מֶלֶךְ הָעוֹלָם, שֶׁהֶחֱיָנוּ וְקִיְּמָנוּ וְהִגִּיעָנוּ
לַזְּמַן הַזֶּה.

Blessed are You, Hashem, our G-d, King of the universe,
Who has kept us alive, sustained us, and brought us to this
season.

We learn from the words "*Zeh Keili V'anveihu*" (This is my G-d and I will glorify Him) that mitzvos should be done beautifully. This includes decorating the sukkah and setting its table nicely.

3
SUKKOS

Sukkos begins on the 15th of Tishrei

Arba'as HaMinim

We make a *brachah* each weekday of Sukkos,
On the *lulav, esrog, hadassim,* and *aravos.*
We study the laws that apply to each kind,
And choose each one with these rules in mind.
We hold in our right hand three of the four;
One *lulav,* two *aravos,* three *hadassim,* no more.
Our left hand holds the *esrog,* up points its stem;
We are ready to say the *brachah* then.
Next, we turn the *esrog's* stem toward the ground,
And in this special order wave the *minim* around:
East, South, West, North, Up, and Down.

*We say this blessing on the Four Species:

בָּרוּךְ אַתָּה ה׳, אֱ–לֹקֵינוּ מֶלֶךְ הָעוֹלָם, אֲשֶׁר קִדְּשָׁנוּ בְּמִצְוֹתָיו,
וְצִוָּנוּ עַל נְטִילַת לוּלָב.

Blessed are You, Hashem, our G-d, King of the universe,
Who has sanctified us with His commandments and
commanded us regarding the taking of the *lulav.*

*The first time, we add this blessing:

בָּרוּךְ אַתָּה ה׳, אֱ–לֹקֵינוּ מֶלֶךְ הָעוֹלָם, שֶׁהֶחֱיָנוּ וְקִיְּמָנוּ וְהִגִּיעָנוּ
לַזְּמַן הַזֶּה.

Blessed are You, Hashem, our G-d, King of the universe,
Who has kept us alive, sustained us, and brought us to this
season.

To fulfill the mitzvah of taking the *lulav,* we must have each of the Four Species: *esrog*
(citron), *lulav* (palm branch), *hadassim* (myrtles), and *aravos* (willow branches).

4 SUKKOS

Sukkos begins on the 15th of Tishrei

Simchas Beis HaSho'eivah

The drawing of water on each Sukkos night,
Began after the *Korban Tamid*, at twilight.
In the *Beis HaMikdash*, young *kohanim* lit lamps of gold,
Which lit up the streets of Yerushalayim of old.
Kohanim sounded their trumpets - each note clear and loud,
While *Levi'im* played instruments and sang before the crowd.
Late into the night *tzaddikim* danced with torches of flame,
They sang songs of praise to Hashem's great Name.
A glow of *kedushah* was seen on each face,
For such joy could be felt in no other place.
Then water was drawn from the Shiloach spring,
And was brought with the morning *Tamid* offering.

This is one of the fifteen "*Shir HaMa'alos*" songs the *Levi'im* sang at the
celebration of the *Simchas Beis HaSho'eivah*:

שִׁיר הַמַּעֲלוֹת, בְּשׁוּב ה' אֶת־שִׁיבַת צִיּוֹן, הָיִינוּ כְּחֹלְמִים. אָז יִמָּלֵא
שְׂחוֹק פִּינוּ וּלְשׁוֹנֵנוּ רִנָּה, אָז יֹאמְרוּ בַגּוֹיִם, הִגְדִּיל ה' לַעֲשׂוֹת עִם־
אֵלֶּה. הִגְדִּיל ה' לַעֲשׂוֹת עִמָּנוּ, הָיִינוּ שְׂמֵחִים...

A song of ascents: When Hashem returns the captivity of
Zion, we will be like dreamers. Then our mouth will be
filled with laughter, and our tongue with glad song. Then
they will declare among the nations, "Hashem has done
greatly with these." Hashem has done greatly with us; we
were gladdened...

"You shall rejoice before Hashem." All the mitzvos of Sukkos are done with joy, but one
who hasn't seen the joy of the *Simchas Beis HaSho'eivah* has never seen real joy.

Sukkos begins on the 15th of Tishrei

Hoshana Rabbah

On *Hoshana Rabbah* night, some people don't go to bed,
They're up learning Torah and saying Tehillim instead.
Our final judgment is sealed on this day;
"Hashem, let the judgment be good!" is what we pray.
When we say *Hoshanos,* five *aravos* are bound,
And then beaten hard five times on the ground.
This *minhag* is from the *Nevi'im's* generation,
And has since been followed by all of our nation.
The *aravos* should then be removed with care,
Because they were used for a mitzvah this year.

*When we take up the *aravos*, we say:

קוֹל מְבַשֵּׂר, מְבַשֵּׂר וְאוֹמֵר; קוֹל מְבַשֵּׂר, מְבַשֵּׂר וְאוֹמֵר; קוֹל מְבַשֵּׂר,
מְבַשֵּׂר וְאוֹמֵר.

The voice of the messenger announces and proclaims!
(three times)

*After beating them, we say:

יְהִי רָצוֹן מִלְפָנֶיךָ, ה׳ אֱ–לֹקֵינוּ וֵא–לֹקֵי אֲבוֹתֵינוּ, הַבּוֹחֵר בַּנְבִיאִים
טוֹבִים וּבְמִנְהֲגֵיהֶם הַטּוֹבִים, שֶׁתְּקַבֵּל בְּרַחֲמִים וּבְרָצוֹן אֶת תְּפִלָּתֵנוּ
וְהַקָפָתֵנוּ...

May it be Your will, Hashem, our G-d and the G-d of our
fathers, Who chooses good prophets and their good
customs, that You accept with mercy and favor our prayers
and our *hakafos*...

On Hoshana Rabbah the whole world is judged for water. *Aravos* grow near water,
and that's why they are used when saying *Hoshanos.*

SHEMINI ATZERES

SIMCHAS TORAH

SHEMINI ATZERES

Shemini Atzeres is on the 22nd of Tishrei

The Prayer for Rain

On Sukkos, Hashem judges the year's rain supply;
He decides: Will it rain, or will it be dry?
But for the Yom Tov of Sukkos we must have dry weather,
Or else, how can we sit in the sukkah together?
So we wait 'til Shemini Atzeres, when we're indoors again,
To ask for the rain by saying "*Morid HaGeshem.*"
"*V'sen Tal U'matar*" is postponed for another few days,
For travelers to the *Beis HaMikdash*, who came from far away.
By the seventh of Marcheshvan*, all were home once more;
So we can daven for rain -- let it rain, let it pour!
All winter we ask for the rain Hashem brings,
Then we switch to a different *Tefilah* in spring.

שָׁאַתָּה הוּא ה' אֱ-לֹקֵינוּ מַשִּׁיב הָרוּחַ וּמוֹרִיד הַגֶּשֶׁם.

For You are Hashem, our G-d,
Who makes the wind blow and the rain fall...

לִבְרָכָה וְלֹא לִקְלָלָה.

*For a blessing, and not a curse.

לְחַיִּים וְלֹא לַמָּוֶת.

*For life, and not death.

לְשֹׂבַע וְלֹא לְרָזוֹן.

*For plenty, and not scarcity.

* Every day from the 22nd of Tishrei until the 15th of Nisan, we say: "מַשִּׁיב הָרוּחַ וּמוֹרִיד הַגֶּשֶׁם" – He makes the wind blow and the rain fall.

"*Morid HaGeshem*" is praise of Hashem. That is why it is said from the 22nd of *Tishrei*.
*Outside of Eretz Yisrael, we begin saying "*V'sen Tal U'matar*" later in the winter, usually around December 4th.

Simchas Torah is on the 23rd of Tishrei *

The Seven *Hakafos*

MY YOM TOV ALBUM

* In Eretz Yisrael, both Shemini Atzeres and Simchas Torah are observed on the 22nd of Tishrei.

Men and boys, young and old alike,
Are waiting to dance with the Torah tonight.
Decorated with silver crowns,
The *sifrei Torah* are passed around.
Kohanim and *Levi'im* are given their chance,
Then all of the other Jews join in the dance.
On Simchas Torah night and day,
The singing is heard from far away.
Seven times around, loud and strong,
We praise Hashem and His Torah in song:

For the First *Hakafah*:
תּוֹרַת ה' תְּמִימָה, מְשִׁיבַת נָפֶשׁ.
*The Torah of Hashem is perfect, restoring the soul.

For the Second *Hakafah*:
עֵדוּת ה' נֶאֱמָנָה, מַחְכִּימַת פֶּתִי.
*The testimony of Hashem is trustworthy, making the simple one wise.

For the Third *Hakafah*:
פִּקּוּדֵי ה' יְשָׁרִים, מְשַׂמְּחֵי־לֵב.
*The orders of Hashem are upright, gladdening the heart.

For the Fourth *Hakafah*:
מִצְוַת ה' בָּרָה, מְאִירַת עֵינָיִם.
*The command of Hashem is clear, enlightening the eyes.

For the Fifth *Hakafah*:
יִרְאַת ה' טְהוֹרָה, עוֹמֶדֶת לָעַד.
*The fear of Hashem is pure, enduring forever.

For the Sixth *Hakafah*:
מִשְׁפְּטֵי ה' אֱמֶת, צָדְקוּ יַחְדָּו.
*The judgments of Hashem are true, altogether righteous.

For the Seventh *Hakafah*:
הַנֶּחֱמָדִים מִזָּהָב וּמִפַּז רָב, וּמְתוּקִים מִדְּבַשׁ וְנֹפֶת צוּפִים.
*They are more desirable than gold, and sweeter than honey.

In the seven *hakafos* we mention the merits of the Seven Shepherds of the Jewish People: Avraham, Yitzchak, Yaakov, Moshe, Aharon, Yosef, and David - the seven *Ushpizin*.

3

SIMCHAS TORAH

Simchas Torah is on the 23rd of Tishrei

Completing the Torah and Starting It Anew

Moshe Rabbeinu taught our nation,
To read the Torah on Shabbos in each generation.
Bereishis, Shemos, Vayikra, Bamidbar, and Devarim,
Are the names of the Torah's five *chumashim*.
We read a parasha each week, as our *Chachamim* said,
And after the parasha, the haftorah is read.
We've read fifty-three parshiyos in the past year,
And on Simchas Torah, the last one we'll hear.
As soon as *"Vezos HaBrachah"* ends,
We turn back and start from *"Bereishis"* again.
The Torah is our greatest treasure,
So we begin it again with joy and with pleasure.

*The final verses of the Torah:

וְזֹאת הַבְּרָכָה אֲשֶׁר בֵּרַךְ מֹשֶׁה אִישׁ הָאֱ–לֹקִים אֶת–בְּנֵי יִשְׂרָאֵל...
וּלְכֹל הַיָּד הַחֲזָקָה וּלְכֹל הַמּוֹרָא הַגָּדוֹל, אֲשֶׁר עָשָׂה מֹשֶׁה לְעֵינֵי כָּל–
יִשְׂרָאֵל.

And this is the blessing that Moshe, the man of G-d, bestowed
on the Children of Israel... And all the mighty acts and great
sights that Moshe displayed before the eyes of all Israel.

*The opening verses:

בְּרֵאשִׁית בָּרָא אֱ–לֹקִים, אֵת הַשָּׁמַיִם וְאֵת הָאָרֶץ... וַיְבָרֶךְ אֱ–לֹקִים
אֶת–יוֹם הַשְּׁבִיעִי וַיְקַדֵּשׁ אֹתוֹ, כִּי בוֹ שָׁבַת מִכָּל–מְלַאכְתּוֹ, אֲשֶׁר–
בָּרָא אֱ–לֹקִים לַעֲשׂוֹת.

In the beginning G-d created the heaven and the earth... And
G-d blessed the seventh day and made it holy, for on it He
rested from all His work, which G-d created to do.

The man called to the Torah for *"Vezos HaBrachah"* is called the *"Chasan Torah."*
The man called to the Torah for *"Bereishis"* is called the *"Chasan Bereishis."*

4

SIMCHAS TORAH

Simchas Torah is on the 23rd of Tishrei

All Are Called to the Torah

50

MY YOM TOV ALBUM

Every man and every boy,
Is called to the Torah on this day of joy.
First is the *Kohen*, the *Levi* is next,
Then come *aliyos* for all of the rest.
Each goes to the *bimah* when his name is called out
And carefully says the *brachah* aloud.
After all say "Amen" the Torah is read,
Then, afterwards, another *brachah* is said.
Another "Amen"; his turn is nearly complete,
He'll soon leave the *bimah* and return to his seat.
When the Torah is finished, and all have taken part,
We begin the Torah once again from the start.

*Before the reading, the one called to the Torah says this blessing:

בָּרוּךְ אַתָּה ה', אֱ–לֹקֵינוּ מֶלֶךְ הָעוֹלָם, אֲשֶׁר בָּחַר בָּנוּ מִכָּל הָעַמִּים,
וְנָתַן לָנוּ אֶת תּוֹרָתוֹ, בָּרוּךְ אַתָּה ה' נוֹתֵן הַתּוֹרָה.

Blessed are You, Hashem, our G-d, King of the universe,
Who chose us from all the peoples and gave us His Torah.
Blessed are You, Hashem, Giver of the Torah.

*After the reading, he says this blessing:

בָּרוּךְ אַתָּה ה', אֱ–לֹקֵינוּ מֶלֶךְ הָעוֹלָם, אֲשֶׁר נָתַן לָנוּ תּוֹרַת אֱמֶת,
וְחַיֵּי עוֹלָם נָטַע בְּתוֹכֵנוּ, בָּרוּךְ אַתָּה ה' נוֹתֵן הַתּוֹרָה.

Blessed are You, Hashem, our G-d, King of the universe,
Who gave us the Torah of truth and implanted eternal life
within us. Blessed are You, Hashem, Giver of the Torah.

In Eretz Yisrael, Shemini Atzeres and Simchas Torah are celebrated the same day.
Outside of Eretz Yisrael, Simchas Torah is celebrated the day after Shemini Atzeres.

5 SIMCHAS TORAH

Simchas Torah is on the 23rd of Tishrei

"Kol HaNe'arim"

All the young boys to the *bimah* are led,
And striped white talleisim are spread overhead.
They stand near the reader, knowing just what to do,
And fathers with babies are there with them too.
Then one man is honored in a special way:
He's called to the Torah with the boys today.
He says the *brachah*, slow and clear;
The boys join in for all to hear.
Next, the Torah reading is heard;
All listen closely to every word.
After the reading, there's a *brachah* again,
And together everyone answers "Amen!"
Then the boys wait, excited and proud,
As the adults say this heartfelt *Tefilah* aloud:

הַמַּלְאָךְ הַגֹּאֵל אֹתִי מִכָּל־רָע, יְבָרֵךְ אֶת־הַנְּעָרִים, וְיִקָּרֵא בָהֶם שְׁמִי
וְשֵׁם אֲבֹתַי אַבְרָהָם וְיִצְחָק, וְיִדְגּוּ לָרֹב בְּקֶרֶב הָאָרֶץ.

May the angel who saves me from all evil *bentch* the boys;
and may my name be declared upon them, along with the
names of my forefathers Avraham and Yitzchak, and may
they increase in the land like fish.

The one called to the Torah for "*Kol HaNe'arim*" must be over bar mitzvah age. He
is called the "*Chasan Me'onah*," because he is called for the reading of "*Me'onah
Elokei Kedem*."

CHANUKAH

CHANUKAH

CHANUKAH

1

Chanukah begins on the 25th of Kislev

Lighting Chanukah Candles

When the sun's rays fade, and day turns to night,
The windows glow with soft candlelight.
We present our father with a special surprise,
And we stand there to watch with sparkling eyes.
A Chanukah menorah; with silver branches tall and straight,
And a *shamash* that stands high above the other eight.
Our father prepares his wicks, one after the other,
And selects colored candles for our little brother.
At the window, two menorahs stand ready;
Father holds Brother's hand firm and steady.
They light the candles when the stars appear,
And recall great miracles from yesteryear.
For thirty minutes, we put work aside,
To celebrate Chanukah with joy and pride.

Before lighting Chanukah candles, we say these blessings:

בָּרוּךְ אַתָּה ה', אֱ–לֹקֵינוּ מֶלֶךְ הָעוֹלָם...

Blessed are You, Hashem, our G-d, King of the universe...

*אֲשֶׁר קִדְּשָׁנוּ בְּמִצְוֹתָיו, וְצִוָּנוּ לְהַדְלִיק נֵר שֶׁל חֲנֻכָּה.

* Who has sanctified us with His commandments and
commanded us to kindle the Chanukah light.

*שֶׁעָשָׂה נִסִּים לַאֲבוֹתֵינוּ, בַּיָּמִים הָהֵם בַּזְּמַן הַזֶּה.

* Who performed miracles for our forefathers in those days, at
this season.

Before lighting the first night, we add this blessing:

*שֶׁהֶחֱיָנוּ וְקִיְּמָנוּ וְהִגִּיעָנוּ לַזְּמַן הַזֶּה.

* Who has kept us alive, sustained us, and brought us to this
season.

To publicize the miracle of Chanukah, we light candles at the front door or
on a windowsill facing the street.

2 CHANUKAH

Chanukah begins on the 25th of Kislev

"Ma'oz Tzur"

Antiochus and his army invaded our land,
And oppressed the Jews with a heavy hand.
Throughout the cities, they announced their decrees:
"Jews who learn Torah will be killed by the Greeks!"
Many were afraid and did as they were told,
They were scared to keep the Torah – its mitzvos to uphold.
Only a handful were courageous and brave,
They went to learn Torah while hiding in caves.
These few served Hashem until they were caught,
And some were killed for the Torah they taught.
Then Mattisyahu defied the decree
And called: "Those who stand with Hashem--come to me!"
Mattisyahu, his five sons, and the Torah-true few,
Fought against those who oppressed every Jew.
Hashem helped the weak win against the strong,
And the Greeks were chased out of our land before long.

After lighting Chanukah candles, we sing:

מָעוֹז צוּר יְשׁוּעָתִי לְךָ נָאֶה לְשַׁבֵּחַ...

Mighty, Rock of my deliverance, to praise You is a delight...

יְוָנִים נִקְבְּצוּ עָלַי אֲזַי בִּימֵי חַשְׁמַנִּים, וּפָרְצוּ חוֹמוֹת מִגְדָּלַי וְטִמְּאוּ כָּל
הַשְּׁמָנִים, וּמִנּוֹתַר קַנְקַנִּים נַעֲשָׂה נֵס לַשּׁוֹשַׁנִּים, בְּנֵי בִינָה יְמֵי שְׁמוֹנָה קָבְעוּ
שִׁיר וּרְנָנִים.

Greeks gathered against me then, in the days of the
Chashmonaim. They breached the walls of my towers and
defiled all the oils. And from the remnant of the flasks, a miracle
was done for the Jews. Men of insight established eight days of
song and jubilation.

To remember the miracles which took place, our Sages established eight days of
Chanukah. The name חנוכה means חנו-כ"ה ה – They rested on the 25th (of Kislev),
the first day of Chanukah.

3 CHANUKAH

Chanukah begins on the 25th of Kislev

"Al HaNissim"

Hashem helped Mattisyahu and his sons,
And the war against the Greeks was finally won.
Now that the enemy had run far, far away,
The Jews could return to the *Beis HaMikdash* to pray.
They thanked Hashem for the victory He gave,
On the twenty-fifth day of the month of Kislev.
But there was still much work to do,
To fix the *Beis HaMikdash* and make it like new.
They purified the *Beis HaMikdash* and all it contains,
The Greek idols were smashed and burned up in flames.
They found one jar of pure oil hidden away–
But it held just enough oil to burn for one day.
They lit the menorah, and their joy was so great,
For the oil burned not just for one day, but eight!
In Chanukah's *bentching* and *Shemoneh Esrei*,
We give thanks for all of these *nissim,* and we say:

In the days of Mattisyahu, the son of Yochanan, the Chashmonai High Priest, and his sons— when the wicked Greek kingdom rose up against Your people, Israel... You in Your great mercy stood up for them in the time of their distress... Thereafter, Your children came to the Holy of Holies of Your house, cleansed Your Temple, purified the site of Your holiness, and kindled lights in the courtyards of Your Sanctuary; and they established these eight days of Chanukah to express thanks and praise to Your great Name.

בִּימֵי מַתִּתְיָהוּ בֶּן יוֹחָנָן כֹּהֵן גָּדוֹל חַשְׁמוֹנָאִי וּבָנָיו, כְּשֶׁעָמְדָה מַלְכוּת יָוָן הָרְשָׁעָה, עַל עַמְּךָ יִשְׂרָאֵל... וְאַתָּה בְּרַחֲמֶיךָ הָרַבִּים, עָמַדְתָּ לָהֶם בְּעֵת צָרָתָם... וְאַחַר כָּךְ בָּאוּ בָנֶיךָ לִדְבִיר בֵּיתֶךָ וּפִנּוּ אֶת הֵיכָלֶךָ וְטִהֲרוּ אֶת מִקְדָּשֶׁךָ וְהִדְלִיקוּ נֵרוֹת בְּחַצְרוֹת קָדְשֶׁךָ וְקָבְעוּ שְׁמוֹנַת יְמֵי חֲנֻכָּה אֵלּוּ לְהוֹדוֹת וּלְהַלֵּל לְשִׁמְךָ הַגָּדוֹל.

On Chanukah we say the entire Hallel, including *"Lo Lanu"* and *"Ahavti Ki Yishma."*

Chanukah begins on the 25th of Kislev

Chanukah Treats

Many and mighty, weapons in hand,
Antiochus and his army waged war in our land.
At first, Jews were killed – they were few and weak –
But Hashem helped the Maccabim defeat the Greeks.
For these miracles – their victorious fight,
And the oil that burned for eight days and nights –
We thank Hashem with song and praise,
And celebrate each year for eight wonderful days.
Chanukah *gelt* is a treat for us all,
We appreciate each gift, no matter how small.
We also like latkes and donuts, hot and sweet,
Served after candle-lighting as a Chanukah treat.

Why are gifts of money given on Chanukah?

The Greeks wanted to destroy the three pillars
upon which the world stands:

Torah, Avodah, and Gemilus Chasadim

Torah, prayer, and acts of kindness.

Therefore, on Chanukah we learn more, pray more, and give more charity. Poor youngsters would collect money door to door, so we give *all* the children *gelt*, in order that the poor not be embarrassed.

On Chanukah we eat fried foods, like latkes and donuts,
to remember the miracle of the jar of pure oil found in the Beis HaMikdash.

5

CHANUKAH

Chanukah begins on the 25th of Kislev

Playing Dreidel

MY YOM TOV ALBUM

"Torah learning is forbidden!" proclaimed the Greeks,
And this was just the first of many decrees.
Announcing Rosh Chodesh, when the moon is new,
And Shabbos and Bris Milah were forbidden too.
But even when the danger of death was near,
Some Jews learned Torah without fear.
The little children were also brave;
They'd learn Torah in secret – deep inside caves.
If the Greeks would find them, the children would say,
"See these tops in our pockets? We came here to play!"
Playing with dreidels was not forbidden,
And in this way they kept their learning hidden.
For Torah they were ready to risk their lives;
They knew without Torah they could not survive.

The letters

nun, gimel, hei, shin

נ , ג , ה , שׁ

On dreidles stand for the words:

נֵס גָּדוֹל הָיָה שָׁם

"A great miracle happened there."

These letters remind us of the miracle even while we play.

In Eretz Yisrael, the dreidels say נ. ג. ה. פ standing for נס גדול היה פה
"A great miracle happened here."

PURIM

PURIM

Purim is on the 14th of Adar *

"Al HaNissim"

MY YOM TOV ALBUM

* In cities which were walled at the time of Yehoshua,
Purim falls on the 15th of Adar. This is called "Shushan Purim."

Haman plotted to wipe out the Jewish nation
And hang Mordechai, the leader of the generation.
Queen Esther fasted and davened for three days,
The Jews of Shushan all followed in her ways.
Then, trembling, she went to Achashverosh on her own,
But he held out his scepter, and she approached the throne.
She invited him and Haman to a party she arranged,
And after that, with Hashem's help, everything changed.
Mordechai was led through Shushan in royal dress,
On the king's own horse, by Haman, no less!
All saw Mordechai honored on that day;
Haman was embarrassed, but he had to obey.
In the end, he and all ten of his sons were killed
And hanged on the gallows his wife had him build.
We thank Hashem for His great *nissim* on this day
In Purim's *bentching* and in *Shemoneh Esrei*:

In the days of Mordechai and Esther, in Shushan, the capital, when wicked Haman rose up against them and tried to destroy, slay, and exterminate all the Jews... You, in Your great mercy, ruined his plan, frustrated his intention, and caused his scheme to backfire. And they hanged him and his sons on the gallows.

בִּימֵי מָרְדְּכַי וְאֶסְתֵּר בְּשׁוּשַׁן הַבִּירָה, כְּשֶׁעָמַד עֲלֵיהֶם הָמָן הָרָשָׁע, בִּקֵּשׁ לְהַשְׁמִיד לַהֲרוֹג וּלְאַבֵּד אֶת כָּל הַיְּהוּדִים... וְאַתָּה בְּרַחֲמֶיךָ הָרַבִּים הֵפַרְתָּ אֶת עֲצָתוֹ, וְקִלְקַלְתָּ אֶת מַחֲשַׁבְתּוֹ, וַהֲשֵׁבוֹתָ לּוֹ גְּמוּלוֹ בְּרֹאשׁוֹ, וְתָלוּ אוֹתוֹ וְאֶת בָּנָיו עַל הָעֵץ.

The miracle of Purim took place in the merit of the fast of Mordechai, Esther, and the entire Jewish people. That's why we fast on the 13th of Adar – *Ta'anis Esther*.

2

PURIM

Purim is on the 14th of Adar

Megillas Esther

On Purim night and in the morning cool,
All are going off to shul.
Children in costume and adults join the crowd
To hear *Megillas Esther* read aloud.
As it is read, the scroll is rolled,
Just like a letter, fold after fold.
All listen closely, paying silent attention,
Except when Haman's name is mentioned.
Each time this *rasha's* name is spoken,
All stamp their feet, and the silence is broken.
Whistles and graggers make more noise,
As Haman's name is "erased" by girls and boys.
We must hear the megillah and not miss a word,
And the *brachos* must also be clearly heard.

Before reading the megillah, the reader says these blessings:

בָּרוּךְ אַתָּה ה', אֱ-לֹקֵינוּ מֶלֶךְ הָעוֹלָם...

Blessed are You, Hashem, our G-d, King of the universe...

*אֲשֶׁר קִדְּשָׁנוּ בְּמִצְוֹתָיו, וְצִוָּנוּ עַל מִקְרָא מְגִלָּה.

*Who has sanctified us with His commandments and commanded
us regarding the reading of the megillah.

*שֶׁעָשָׂה נִסִּים לַאֲבוֹתֵינוּ בַּיָּמִים הָהֵם בַּזְּמַן הַזֶּה.

*Who performed miracles for our forefathers in those days, at this
season.

*שֶׁהֶחֱיָנוּ וְקִיְּמָנוּ וְהִגִּיעָנוּ לַזְּמַן הַזֶּה.

*Who has kept us alive, sustained us, and brought us to this season.

Haman was a descendant of Amalek, and we are commanded to "erase the memory of Amalek." That's why we make noise when Haman's name is mentioned in the megillah.

3

PURIM

Purim is on the 14th of Adar

The Purim *Seudah*

After the Purim feast we were pleased,
For this was a mitzvah earned with ease.
With Purim's four mitzvos done for the year,
We knew we could start to drink wine without fear.
A drunk is usually silly and sad,
But drinking on Purim is not something bad.
It's a mitzvah to drink some wine on this day,
Our father filled up his cup – all the way!
He stopped when Mommy said, "Please, no more!"
But he was already a little drunk from before.
Who's Haman? Who's Mordechai? He just couldn't say,
So we knew that he'd drunk enough for the day.

חַיָּב אָדָם לְבַסּוּמֵי בְּפוּרַיָּא, עַד דְּלֹא יָדַע בֵּין אָרוּר הָמָן לְבָרוּךְ מָרְדְּכַי.

One is obligated to drink on Purim until he cannot tell the difference between "cursed is Haman" and "blessed is Mordechai."

*The source of the mitzvah:

Mordechai recorded these events and sent letters to all the Jews... telling them to observe the fourteenth and fifteenth of Adar every year... They were to celebrate them as days of **feasting and gladness**...

וַיִּכְתֹּב מָרְדְּכַי אֶת־הַדְּבָרִים הָאֵלֶּה,
וַיִּשְׁלַח סְפָרִים אֶל־כָּל־הַיְּהוּדִים,
אֲשֶׁר בְּכָל־מְדִינוֹת הַמֶּלֶךְ אֲחַשְׁוֵרוֹשׁ,
הַקְּרוֹבִים וְהָרְחוֹקִים, לְקַיֵּם עֲלֵיהֶם
לִהְיוֹת עֹשִׂים אֵת יוֹם אַרְבָּעָה עָשָׂר
לְחֹדֶשׁ אֲדָר וְאֵת יוֹם־חֲמִשָּׁה עָשָׂר בּוֹ,
בְּכָל־שָׁנָה וְשָׁנָה... יְמֵי מִשְׁתֶּה
וְשִׂמְחָה...

We drink wine on Purim to remember the miracles, which all began at parties with wine: Vashti was executed, Esther was made queen, and Haman had his downfall.

4
PURIM

Purim is on the 14th of Adar

Mishloach Manos

Inside, outside, all around,
Joyous Purim sights are found.
Beautiful costumes, all colors and sizes,
And baskets packed with Purim surprises.
The baskets are full of drinks and food,
Cake and some wine for a Purim mood!
In our yard, I saw the funniest sight:
A huge brown bear marching upright!
He held the biggest basket ever,
As if it were as light as a feather.
He hurried to bring it to his best friend,
Before the sun sets, when Purim would end.

*The source of the mitzvah:

Mordechai recorded these events and sent letters to all the Jews... telling them to observe the fourteenth and fifteenth of Adar every year... They were to celebrate them as days of feasting and gladness, **sending treats to one another...**

וַיִּכְתֹּב מָרְדֳּכַי אֶת־הַדְּבָרִים הָאֵלֶּה, וַיִּשְׁלַח סְפָרִים אֶל־כָּל־הַיְּהוּדִים, אֲשֶׁר בְּכָל־מְדִינוֹת הַמֶּלֶךְ אֲחַשְׁוֵרוֹשׁ, הַקְּרוֹבִים וְהָרְחוֹקִים, לְקַיֵּם עֲלֵיהֶם לִהְיוֹת עֹשִׂים אֵת יוֹם אַרְבָּעָה עָשָׂר לְחֹדֶשׁ אֲדָר וְאֵת יוֹם־חֲמִשָּׁה עָשָׂר בּוֹ, בְּכָל־שָׁנָה וְשָׁנָה... יְמֵי מִשְׁתֶּה וְשִׂמְחָה וּמִשְׁלֹחַ מָנוֹת אִישׁ לְרֵעֵהוּ...

On Purim, everyone must send at least two portions of food to one person. A "portion" means food that is ready to eat, like cooked dishes, candy, or pastry.

PURIM

Purim is on the 14th of Adar

Mattanos La'Evyonim

In a yard far away from the nicer homes,
A poor child sat, sad and alone.
Two playful chickens jumped on his seat
And pecked at the torn, old shoes on his feet.
Even on Purim, he was so very sad
That just the sight of him made me feel bad.
But when I gave him a Purim surprise,
New light began to shine in his eyes.
I still had one more place to go,
To another poor family that we know.
By giving two gifts of *tzedakah* that day,
I celebrated Purim the proper way.

*The source of the mitzvah:

Mordechai recorded these events and sent letters to all the Jews... telling them to observe the fourteenth and fifteenth of Adar every year... They were to celebrate them as days of feasting and gladness, sending treats to one another, and **gifts to the poor.**

וַיִּכְתֹּב מָרְדֳּכַי אֶת־הַדְּבָרִים הָאֵלֶּה, וַיִּשְׁלַח סְפָרִים אֶל־כָּל־הַיְּהוּדִים, אֲשֶׁר בְּכָל־מְדִינוֹת הַמֶּלֶךְ אֲחַשְׁוֵרוֹשׁ, הַקְּרוֹבִים וְהָרְחוֹקִים, לְקַיֵּם עֲלֵיהֶם לִהְיוֹת עֹשִׂים אֵת יוֹם אַרְבָּעָה עָשָׂר לְחֹדֶשׁ אֲדָר וְאֵת יוֹם־חֲמִשָּׁה עָשָׂר בּוֹ, בְּכָל־שָׁנָה וְשָׁנָה... יְמֵי מִשְׁתֶּה וְשִׂמְחָה וּמִשְׁלֹחַ מָנוֹת אִישׁ לְרֵעֵהוּ, וּמַתָּנוֹת לָאֶבְיֹנִים.

It is a mitzvah to give charity to at least two poor people on Purim. Everyone, even a poor person who receives charity himself, must fulfill this mitzvah.

PESACH

PESACH

Pesach begins on the 15th of Nisan

Selling the *Chametz*

Look at our kitchen, see what we've got:
Silverware, glasses, dishes, and pots.
For dairy and for meat, two of each kind,
Different in color, in form and design.
Before Pesach, we scrub them all clean,
And pack them away where they won't be seen.
But even with the house sparkling and neat,
Our Pesach work is not yet complete.
Throughout the Pesach holiday,
We can't own *chametz* in any way.
So the very next thing that we have to do,
Is to sell our *chametz* to a non-Jew.
Our rabbi will usually sell it for us,
But we can do it ourselves if we must.

"בַּל יֵרָאֶה וּבַל יִמָּצֵא"

"(*Chametz*) must not be seen or found"

We may not own any *chametz* on Pesach, so we either burn our *chametz* or sell it to a non-Jew. We do not sell our dishes, only whatever *chametz* they may contain.

After Pesach we need not immerse our dishes in a *mikveh* as we do with dishes bought from a non-Jew, since we sold only the *chametz* absorbed in them, and not the dishes themselves.

2 PESACH

Pesach begins on the 15th of Nisan

Searching for *Chametz*

Our whole house is really spotless tonight,
The dining room and kitchen are clean and bright.
We have no *chametz* anymore,
Just a small bag put away near the door.
Ten bits of bread, well wrapped but small,
Are carefully placed in the rooms and the hall.
As soon as it's dark, and the stars appear,
Our father makes a *brachah* loud and clear.
Then he checks to see if he will find,
Any *chametz* that was left behind.
By candlelight we search together,
As he gathers the crumbs with a spoon and feather.

*Before searching for *chametz*, we say this blessing:

בָּרוּךְ אַתָּה ה׳, אֱ–לֹקֵינוּ מֶלֶךְ הָעוֹלָם, אֲשֶׁר קִדְּשָׁנוּ בְּמִצְוֹתָיו, וְצִוָּנוּ עַל בִּעוּר חָמֵץ.

Blessed are You, Hashem, our G-d, King of the universe, Who has sanctified us with His commandments and commanded us regarding the removal of *chametz*.

*Afterwards we say:

כָּל חֲמִירָא וַחֲמִיעָא דְּאִכָּא בִרְשׁוּתִי, דְּלָא חֲמִתֵּהּ וּדְלָא בִעַרְתֵּהּ וּדְלָא יְדַעְנָא לֵהּ, לִבָּטֵל וְלֶהֱוֵי הֶפְקֵר כְּעַפְרָא דְאַרְעָא.

Any *chametz* or leaven in my possession that I have not seen, have not removed, and do not know about, should be annulled and become ownerless, like dust of the earth.

Ten small pieces of bread are hidden around the house, so the blessing ״עַל בעור חמץ״ will not be in vain if no other *chametz* is found.

3
PESACH

Pesach begins on the 15th of Nisan

Burning the *Chametz*

MY YOM TOV ALBUM

In the bare field where we like to play,
Our father lit a special fire today.
We threw in the bread that he had found
In last night's search, scattered around.
Next came our pretzels and crackers and cake,
And the rest of the cookies that Mommy had baked.
The last thing to go in was our sandwich crusts;
The fire burned them to ashes and dust.
On Pesach, no *chametz* may be seen or found,
Even if it's only a tiny amount.
Plain, or mixed with food in any way,
It's strictly forbidden for the next eight* days.

*In Eretz Yisrael, Pesach is celebrated for only seven days.

After burning the *chametz*, we say:

כָּל חֲמִירָא וַחֲמִיעָא דְּאִכָּא בִרְשׁוּתִי, דַּחֲזִתֵּהּ וּדְלָא חֲזִתֵּהּ, דְּחָמִתֵּהּ
וּדְלָא חֲמִתֵּהּ, דְּבִעַרְתֵּהּ וּדְלָא בִעַרְתֵּהּ, לִבָּטֵל וְלֶהֱוֵי הֶפְקֵר כְּעַפְרָא
דְּאַרְעָא.

Any *chametz* or leaven in my possession – whether I have
seen it or not, whether I have removed it or not – should be
annulled and become ownerless, like dust of the earth.

Chametz found on *Chol HaMoed* must be burned. If it is found on *Yom Tov* or on
Shabbos, it should be covered until after *Havdalah*, then burned.

4

PESACH

Pesach begins on the 15th of Nisan

The Seder

MY YOM TOV ALBUM

Like kings and queens, dressed in our best,
We sit down to the Seder with our guests.
Beautiful *bechers* we prepare
Along with Haggados for everyone here.
The big polished silver *kos* that you see,
Is ready to be used by Eliyahu HaNavi.
The *ke'arah* is a most impressive sight,
Set with the symbols of the Seder night.
Father puts three *shemurah matzos* inside,
Then breaks the middle one and puts half aside.
The child who finds the piece that was hidden away
Gets an *afikoman* gift for the holiday.
About wine, *maror*, *matzah*, and other new sights,
The children will ask many questions tonight:

מַה נִּשְׁתַּנָּה הַלַּיְלָה הַזֶּה מִכָּל הַלֵּילוֹת.

Why is this night different from all other nights?

*שֶׁבְּכָל הַלֵּילוֹת אָנוּ אוֹכְלִין חָמֵץ וּמַצָּה, הַלַּיְלָה הַזֶּה כֻּלּוֹ מַצָּה.

*On all other nights we may eat *chametz* and *matzah*,
but on this night only *matzah*.

*שֶׁבְּכָל הַלֵּילוֹת אָנוּ אוֹכְלִין שְׁאָר יְרָקוֹת, הַלַּיְלָה הַזֶּה מָרוֹר.

*On all other nights we eat many vegetables, but on this night we eat *maror*.

*שֶׁבְּכָל הַלֵּילוֹת אֵין אָנוּ מַטְבִּילִין אֲפִלּוּ פַּעַם אֶחָת, הַלַּיְלָה הַזֶּה שְׁתֵּי פְעָמִים.

*On all other nights we do not dip even once, but on this night we dip twice.

*שֶׁבְּכָל הַלֵּילוֹת אָנוּ אוֹכְלִין בֵּין יוֹשְׁבִין וּבֵין מְסֻבִּין, הַלַּיְלָה הַזֶּה כֻּלָּנוּ מְסֻבִּין.

*On all other nights we eat sitting or reclining,
but on this night we all recline.

The children should be encouraged to ask the Four Questions, and the adults should
answer them. The more we tell about *Yetzias Mitzrayim* by the Seder, the better.

5

PESACH

Pesach begins on the 15th of Nisan

The Prayer for *Tal* (Dew)

On Pesach, Hashem judges
how much wheat we'll have this year,
Now that it is spring, and the harvest time is near.
In spring, we don't ask Hashem for rain,
For water would spoil the ripened grain.
By now the wheat has already grown tall,
So instead, we ask for dew to fall.
On the first day of Pesach, each year anew,
We praise Hashem with the *Tefilah* for dew.
Some say "*Morid HaTal*" in *Shemoneh Esrei*,
So the fields will be covered with dew every day.
We'll say "*V'sen Brachah*" until fall comes again,
When we'll daven for rain, which is needed then.

In the prayer for dew, we say:

שָׁאַתָּה הוּא ה' אֱ–לֹקֵינוּ מַשִּׁיב הָרוּחַ וּמוֹרִיד הַטָּל.

For You are Hashem, our G-d, Who makes the wind
blow and the dew fall.

לִבְרָכָה וְלֹא לִקְלָלָה.

*For a blessing, and not a curse.

לְחַיִּים וְלֹא לַמָּוֶת.

*For life, and not death.

לְשֹׂבַע וְלֹא לְרָזוֹן.

*For plenty, and not scarcity.

Every day from the 15th of Nisan until the 22nd of Tishrei, we say: "מוֹרִיד הַטָּל" – He makes the Dew fall.

The Torah tells us, "You will count from the day after Shabbos, from the day you bring the Omer offering." In the merit of the Omer offering brought on Pesach, the crops are blessed.

Pesach begins on the 15th of Nisan

Sefiras Ha'Omer

Body and soul, the Jews were enslaved,
Then with great miracles they were saved.
In Mitzrayim they sank as low as can be–
But Hashem redeemed them and made them free.
In the *midbar*, Hashem prepared them – heart and soul,
To receive the Torah – for that was the goal.
The Jews waited eagerly, counting each day,
So now we count *Sefirah* the very same way:
For seven full weeks, as the Torah commands,
Each day a *brachah* is said beforehand.
If we forget to count with a *brachah* at night,
We count, with no *brachah*, next day when it's light.
Yet our nation is sad during these days,
As we mourn for great scholars who passed away.
Rabbi Akiva's students lacked some respect for each other,
And didn't show enough honor for one another.
Each year we mourn their deaths anew,
And resolve to respect our fellow Jew.

Between Pesach and Shavuos every evening after *Ma'ariv*, we make a blessing and count that day's *Sefiras Ha'Omer*.

בָּרוּךְ אַתָּה ה', אֱ–לֹקֵינוּ מֶלֶךְ הָעוֹלָם, אֲשֶׁר קִדְּשָׁנוּ בְּמִצְוֹתָיו, וְצִוָּנוּ עַל סְפִירַת הָעוֹמֶר.

Blessed are You, Hashem, our G-d, King of the universe, Who has sanctified us with His commandments and commanded us regarding the counting of the Omer.

Lag Ba'Omer, the 33rd day of the Omer, is a joyous day because Rabbi Akiva's students stopped dying on this day. It's also the *Yahrzeit* of the saintly *tanna*, Rabbi Shimon bar Yochai, who is buried in Meron.

SHAVUOS

SHAVUOS

① SHAVUOS

Shavuos is on the 6th of Sivan

Decorating the House with Greenery

We welcome Shavuos in a beautiful way,
By decorating the house for this special day;
With branches and leaves and flowers in bloom
On the walls and the windows of every room.
On the Yom Tov table, set for tonight,
Is a vase filled with flowers – pink, red, and white.
The main reason that we do this all
Is to remember Har Sinai, humble and small.
It bloomed with grass, flowers, and leaves everywhere,
When Hashem gave us the holy Torah there.
Another *minhag* often seen,
Is decorating the shul with all kinds of greens.

The custom and its source:

Before Shavuos, homes and synagogues are decorated with greenery to recall Har Sinai, which was covered with grass. We know this from the warning given to Moshe Rabbeinu before the Torah was given:

"גַּם־הַצֹּאן וְהַבָּקָר אַל־יִרְעוּ אֶל־מוּל הָהָר הַהוּא"

"Even the sheep and the cattle may not graze near the mountain."

Moshe was born on the 7th of Adar, then hidden for three months. On the 6th of Sivan, he was put in the reeds near the Nile. We remember this event as well with greenery.

Shavuos is on the 6th of Sivan

Learning All Night

MY YOM TOV ALBUM

The *seudah* is over and now all the men
Return with the boys to shul once again.
While the women and girls are asleep for the night,
The shuls are alive with noise and with light.
Everyone joins in Torah learning;
Hour after hour, the pages keep turning.
After a whole night spent this way,
It's as if the Torah were given today.
Tikun Leil Shavuos is said on this night,
Until the men see that it's getting light.
They thank Hashem, Who chose our nation
To be His people for all generations.

Before learning, we say:

אַתָּה בְחַרְתָּנוּ מִכָּל הָעַמִּים, אָהַבְתָּ אוֹתָנוּ וְרָצִיתָ בָּנוּ... וַתִּתֶּן לָנוּ ה׳
אֱ-לֹקֵינוּ הַתּוֹרָה הַקְּדוֹשָׁה וְחֻקִּים הַיְשָׁרִים בְּהַר סִינַי בַּיּוֹם הַקָּדוֹשׁ
הַזֶּה. וַתְּצַוֵּנוּ ה׳ אֱ-לֹקֵינוּ לַהֲגוֹת בְּאִמְרֵי תוֹרָתֶךָ יוֹמָם וָלָיְלָה, כִּי
הֵם חַיֵּינוּ וְאֹרֶךְ יָמֵינוּ...

You have chosen us from all the peoples; You loved us and
found favor in us... and You gave us, Hashem, our G-d...
the holy Torah and upright laws on Har Sinai on this holy
day. And You commanded us, Hashem, our G-d, to learn
the words of Your Torah day and night, because they are
our life and the length of our days...

The day the Torah was given, the Jewish people slept late and had to be awakened.
To make amends, men stay up all night on Shavuos and learn Torah.

Shavuos is on the 6th of Sivan

Megillas Rus

There was terrible hunger in the land,
And Elimelech was asked to open his hand.
Rich as he was, he chose not to give,
He went to the fields of Moav to live.
He took his wife Naomi and their two sons along,
But he and his sons passed away before long.
Naomi and her daughters-in-law were left alone,
So Naomi decided it was time to go home.
Her daughter-in-law, Rus, insisted on coming too,
For she was determined to become a Jew.
Rus was rewarded for what she had done;
Dovid, our king, was her great grandson.
That's one reason we read *Megillas Rus* today:
On Shavuos, Dovid HaMelech was born and passed away.

When the megillah is read from a parchment scroll, some say these blessings:

בָּרוּךְ אַתָּה ה', אֱ–לֹקֵינוּ מֶלֶךְ הָעוֹלָם...

Blessed are You, Hashem, our G-d, King of the universe...

*אֲשֶׁר קִדְּשָׁנוּ בְּמִצְוֹתָיו, וְצִוָּנוּ עַל מִקְרָא מְגִלָּה.

*Who has sanctified us with His commandments and commanded us regarding the reading of the megillah.

*שֶׁהֶחֱיָנוּ וְקִיְּמָנוּ וְהִגִּיעָנוּ לַזְּמַן הַזֶּה.

*Who has kept us alive, sustained us, and brought us to this season.

Our Sages asked: Why is *Megillas Rus* read on Shavuos? Because we learn from Rus that the Torah can be acquired only through poverty and suffering.

Shavuos is on the 6th of Sivan

Eating Dairy Foods

The Shavuos table is set with our best,
But this meal is different from the rest.
Instead of fish, soup, and meat,
Our mother serves us dairy treats:
Blintzes and kugels with milk and cheese,
And creamy pudding that's sure to please.
Our favorite is the fluffy cheesecake,
Which only Mommy knows how to bake.
There's a reason for the dairy foods we eat:
When the Jews got the Torah, they couldn't eat meat.
They learned that their dishes were non-kosher before,
So they could not use these dishes anymore.
But because it was Shabbos when the Torah was received,
They couldn't *kasher* the dishes that they would need.

Another reason for the custom:

The Torah is compared to milk and honey:

‎"דְּבַשׁ וְחָלָב תַּחַת לְשׁוֹנֵךְ"

"Honey and milk are under your tongue."

That's why we eat foods with milk and honey on the
day the Torah was received.

When the Torah was given, the Jews learned that milk is not considered part of a
living animal, so starting that day, they began to eat dairy products.

Shavuos is on the 6th of Sivan

Aliyah LaRegel

Pesach, Shavuos, and Sukkos – three times a year–
Jews would come to the *Beis HaMikdash* from far and near.
Korbanos were brought for each holiday,
But we have no *Beis HaMikdash* today.
All that is left is the western wall,
Which survived our enemies, one and all.
The Kosel still stands to this very day,
And Jews from all over come there to pray:
"Please rebuild Your *Beis HaMikdash*, Hashem!
Let it never be destroyed again!"
The third *Beis HaMikdash* will stand forever,
And there we will serve Hashem, all together.

The Torah tells us three times:

שָׁלוֹשׁ פְּעָמִים בַּשָּׁנָה יֵרָאֶה כָּל־זְכוּרְךָ אֶת־פְּנֵי ה' אֱ–לֹקֶיךָ... בְּחַג
הַמַּצּוֹת וּבְחַג הַשָּׁבֻעוֹת וּבְחַג הַסֻּכּוֹת, וְלֹא יֵרָאֶה אֶת־פְּנֵי ה' רֵיקָם:
אִישׁ כְּמַתְּנַת יָדוֹ, כְּבִרְכַּת ה' אֱ–לֹקֶיךָ אֲשֶׁר נָתַן־לָךְ.

Three times a year, all your males are to appear before
Hashem, your G-d... on the festival of *matzos*, on the
festival of Shavuos, and on the festival of Sukkos, and
they shall not appear before Hashem empty-handed.
Every man according to the gift of his hand, according to
the blessing of Hashem.

לְשָׁנָה הַבָּאָה בִּירוּשָׁלַיִם הַבְּנוּיָה

Next Year in Jerusalem

The earliest time for bringing *bikkurim* (first fruit) is on Shavuos. This mitzvah
can be fulfilled only when we have a *Beis HaMikdash*.

GLOSSARY

All entries are Hebrew terms unless otherwise indicated. Words defined in the text or appearing in a standard English-language dictionary have been omitted.

* ACHASHVEROSH – wicked Persian king in MEGILLAS ESTHER
* AFIKOMAN – (Aramaic) final *matzah* eaten at the Seder
* AHAVTI KI YISHMA – "I have loved [HASHEM], for He will hear"; opening phrase of TEHILLIM 116
* AKEIDAS YITZCHAK – the binding of Isaac (BEREISHIS 22)
* ALIYAH – (lit. "ascent") going up to the BIMAH to read the Torah
* ANTIOCHUS – Greek king who tried to destroy the Jews and whose defeat is celebrated on Chanukah
* ARBA'AS HAMINIM – the four species
* AVEIRAH/AVEIROS – sin(s)
* BA'AL TOKE'A – one who blows the shofar on Rosh Hashanah
* BAMIDBAR – (lit. "in the wilderness") the Book of Numbers
* BARUCH HASHEM – "thank G-d"
* BECHER – (Yiddish) goblet
* BEIS HAMIKDASH – the Temple
* BENTCH – (Yiddish) to bless
* BENTCHING – (Yiddish) reciting the Grace after Meals
* BEREISHIS – (lit. "in the beginning") the book of Genesis; the name of the first portion therein
* BRACHAH / BRACHOS – blessing(s)
* CHAMETZ – leaven, forbidden on Pesach
* ME'ONAH ELOKEI KEDEM – "the eternal G-d is a dwelling place" (DEVARIM 33:27)
* CHOL HAMO'ED – intermediate days of the festivals
* CHUMASHIM – the Five Books of Moses
* DEVARIM – (lit. "words") The Book of Deuteronomy
* ERETZ YISRAEL – the Land of Israel
* EREV PESACH – Pesach eve
* EREV YOM KIPPUR – Yom Kippur eve
* GEZEIROS – decrees
* GRAGGERS – (Yiddish) noisemakers
* HAKAFAH(OS) – circuits around the BIMAH on Simchas Torah
* HAR SINAI – Mount Sinai, where the Torah was given
* HASHEM – (lit. "the Name") G-d
* HAVDALAH – (lit. "separation") concluding ceremony of SHABBOS
* HOSHANA RABBAH – last day of Sukkos, devoted to penitential prayers and beating *aravos*
* HOSHANOS – (lit. "please save") penitential prayers said on HOSHANA RABBAH
* KE'ARAH – Seder plate
* KEDUSHAH – holiness
* KOHEN / KOHANIM – member(s) of the priestly dynasty

* KOL HANE'ARIM – "all the youths"
* KORBAN / KORBANOS – sacrifice(s) offered in the BEIS HAMIKDASH
* KOS – goblet
* LASHON HARA – evil speech
* LO LANU – "Not for us"; opening phrase of TEHILLIM 115
* MACHZORIM – holiday prayer books
* MARCHESHVAN – 2nd month of the Jewish calendar
* MAROR – bitter herb eaten at the Seder to remind us of our bitter enslavement in Egypt
* MEGILLAS ESTHER – scroll containing the Book of Esther
* MEGILLAS RUS – scroll containing the Book of Ruth
* MIDBAR – desert
* MIKVEH – ritual bath
* MINHAG – custom
* MISHPACHAH – family
* MOSHE RABBEINU – the biblical Moses, our teacher
* RASHA – wicked person
* SATAN – adversary
* S'CHACH – thatched roof of a sukkah
* SEFIRAS HA'OMER – the counting of the Omer
* SELICHOS – penitential prayers said before and after Rosh Hashanah
* SEUDAH – festive meal
* SHABBOS – the Sabbath; Talmudic tractate concerning this day
* SHAMASH – (lit. "servant") candle used to light the Chanukah menorah
* SHEMONEH ESREI – (lit. "eighteen") main prayer of the daily liturgy,
  which originally contained eighteen blessings
* SHEMOS – (lit. "names") the book of Exodus
* SHEMURAH MATZOS – *matzos* made from wheat guarded since the harvest to ensure
  that it never became CHAMETZ; eaten at the Seder
* SIFREI TORAH – Torah scrolls
* SIMCHAS BEIS HASHO'EIVAH – "celebration at the place of the drawing of water"
* TEFILAH – prayer
* TEHILLIM – Psalms
* TESHUVAH – repentance
* TIKUN LEIL SHAVUOS – special selections studied on Shavuos night
* TZEDAKAH – charity
* USHPIZIN – (Aramaic) (lit. "guests") seven biblical figures invited into the sukkah each
  night of Sukkos
* VAYIKRA – (lit. "He called") the Book of Leviticus
* VEZOS HABRACHAH – (lit. "and this is the blessing") concluding portion of the Torah
  (DEVARIM 33-34)
* YEHI RATZON – a prayer request, i.e. "May it be Your will..."
* YETZIAS MITZRAYIM – the exodus from Egypt

MY YOM TOV
ALBUM

MY YOM TOV
ALBUM

MY YOM TOV
ALBUM

MY YOM TOV
ALBUM

MY YOM TOV
ALBUM

MY YOM TOV
ALBUM

MY YOM TOV
ALBUM

MY YOM TOV
ALBUM

MY YOM TOV
ALBUM

MY YOM TOV
ALBUM

MY YOM TOV
ALBUM

MY YOM TOV
ALBUM

MY YOM TOV
ALBUM

MY YOM TOV
ALBUM

MY YOM TOV
ALBUM

MY YOM TOV
ALBUM

MY YOM TOV
ALBUM